Connelly, Elizabeth Russell.

Nicotine = busted!

MEDIA CENTER
ST. JOSEPH GRADE SCHOOL

Nicotine

Elizabeth Russell Connelly

Enslow Publishers, Inc.
40 Industrial Road
Box 398
Berkeley Heights, NJ 07922
USA

http://www.enslow.com

Library of Congress Cataloging-in-Publication Data

Connelly, Elizabeth Russell.
 Nicotine=Busted! / Elizabeth Russell Connelly.
  p. cm. — (Busted!)
 Includes bibliographical references and index.
 ISBN 0-7660-2473-3
  1. Nicotine addiction—Juvenile literature. 2. Nicotine—Juvenile literature.
 3. Smoking—Juvenile literature. 4. Youth—Tobacco use—Juvenile literature. I. Title.
 II. Series.
 HV5740.C66   2006
 613.85—dc22
                                                    2005029373

Printed in the United States of America

10 9 8 7 6 5 4 3 2 1

To Our Readers:
We have done our best to make sure all Internet Addresses in this book were active and
appropriate when we went to press. However, the author and the publisher have no control
over and assume no liability for the material available on those Internet sites or on other Web
sites they may link to. Any comments or suggestions can be sent by e-mail to
comments@enslow.com or to the address on the back cover.

Every effort has been made to locate all copyright holders of material used in this book. If any
errors or omissions have occurred, corrections will be made in future editions of this book.

Illustration Credits: Associated Press, pp. 12, 14, 35; Associated Press, The Advocate-
Messenger, pp. 28–29; Associated Press, Alamogordo Daily News, p. 60; BananaStock, pp.
4–5, 66–67; Department of Health and Human Resources, Centers for Disease Control and
Prevention, p. 89; DigitalStock, pp. 16–17, 43, 48–49, 63, 69; ©2006 Jupiterimages, pp. 26, 31
(inset), 33, 37, 83, 91; National Cancer Institute, p. 55; Courtesy of the National Institute on
Drug Abuse, p. 20; Shutterstock, p. 31 (background); stockbyte, pp. 9, 57, 78–79; U.S.
Department of Health & Human Services, pp. 39, 75.

Cover Illustration: Shutterstock.

CONTENTS

CHAPTER ONE

THE LANDSCAPE

Patrolling the city's west side just after midnight, Officer John Wheeler of the San Antonio, Texas, Police Department slowed down to investigate a car parked on the side of the road.[1]

"I noticed the brake lights going off and on, and I thought it looked suspicious," explained Wheeler. "As I pulled up behind it, I could see five kids sitting in the car."[2]

Wheeler walked up to the driver's side, and shined his flashlight into the car. "I asked them what they were doing," reported Wheeler. "One of the boys said they were going to their friend's house to play video games. When I asked him where their friend lived, he said he didn't know."[3]

Because the kids seemed nervous and their stories did not add up, Wheeler decided to probe a little further. He called for backup. Once the other officers arrived, they approached the car from both sides, flashlights in hand. They asked everyone for identification, which revealed that the boys were between fifteen and seventeen years old.

The officers also detected the smell of cigarette smoke in the car. The legal age for smoking in the United States is eighteen years old. If these boys had been smoking, they were breaking the law.

The officers asked the teens to get out of the car while they searched it. "We found a pack of rolling papers, which made us suspect they were either using or looking for marijuana. None was in the car. However," noted Wheeler, "we also found a pack of cigarettes with one cigarette left."[4]

At first, no one wanted to claim responsibility. Then one of the fifteen-year-old boys told the officers that the pack belonged to him. He said that a friend had given it to him. Because the boy was underage, Wheeler wrote him a citation for possession of tobacco. He told the teen that his parents and he would have to appear in court and pay a fine. According to Texas law, that fine could be up to $200. And that is only the beginning. The boy will probably also be put on probation, do community service, and attend a tobacco-education class. Because tobacco laws vary state to state, he might have faced different or more severe penalties elsewhere.

What Is Nicotine?

Nicotine is an addictive drug—as addictive as heroin and cocaine. It is found in small amounts in certain plants, but most commonly in the tobacco plant. Nicotine makes up about 5 percent of a tobacco plant by weight.[5] Basically, tobacco is nicotine's delivery truck.

A person gets nicotine into his or her system through either smoking or smokeless tobacco.

The most common forms of smoking tobacco are cigarettes, cigars, and loose pipe tobacco. Some kids get their first shot of nicotine by smoking bidis and kreteks, which are flavored cigarettes. Smokeless tobacco comes in two forms—chew and snuff—but it is often also called dip, chaw, plug, and spit tobacco. Because there is no burning cigarette or cloud of smoke, some people believe that using chew or snuff is safer than smoking. But tobacco in any form can cause heart disease and cancer. Cigarettes and cigars are more likely to cause lung cancer, while chew and snuff usually lead to mouth, throat, and stomach cancers. Among eighth-graders in 2005, about 26 percent say they have smoked cigarettes, while 10 percent have tried smokeless tobacco. The same survey showed that only a fraction of a percentage had tried bidis or kreteks.[6]

Smoking Tobacco

Cigarettes are made of finely shredded tobacco wrapped in a narrow tube of paper. Most have a filter tip, which is intended to reduce the amount of tar and nicotine a smoker inhales. Cigars are made from air-cured or dried tobacco that has been aged and fermented for one to two years.

Cigarettes are made of finely shredded tobacco wrapped in paper. Most have a filter tip to reduce the amounts of tar and nicotine inhaled.

The fermentation causes chemical and bacterial reactions that change the tobacco and give cigars a different taste and smell from cigarettes.

When someone smokes a cigarette or cigar, he or she gets more than nicotine. An unlit cigarette contains more than sixty chemicals that can cause cancer.[7] Light that cigarette, and the smoke it produces contains about four thousand different chemicals.[8] Many of these are added by tobacco producers to make their products more addictive and more flavorful. Ammonia is one example. It boosts the effect of nicotine up to one hundred times. Some added chemicals also increase the rate at which a cigarette burns. The faster it burns, the more packs of cigarettes a smoker will buy.

Some kids think flavored cigarettes—which include bidis and kreteks—are safer than smoking regular cigarettes. In some ways, these kinds are worse. For instance, bidis are unfiltered and contain about 28 percent more nicotine than regular cigarettes.[9]

Bidis are imported mainly from India. They are hand-rolled in a leaf and tied with strings on the ends. Bidis contain less tobacco than regular cigarettes, but still contain tar, carbon monoxide, and other harmful substances. They come in colorful packages and have candylike flavors. They are usually less expensive than regular cigarettes and give smokers an immediate buzz. Thinner than regular cigarettes, they require about three times as many puffs per cigarette.[10] Because they are unfiltered, all those dangerous chemicals get sucked in by the smoker. According to a study done in India, bidi smokers have nearly four times the risk of chronic bronchitis than nonsmokers.[11]

Kreteks are Indonesian clove cigarettes, which deliver more nicotine, carbon monoxide, and tar than regular cigarettes.[12] Kreteks contain about 70 percent tobacco and 30 percent ground cloves, clove oil, and other additives. Research in Indonesia has shown that regular kretek smokers put themselves at up to twenty times the risk for abnormal lung function.[13]

Some teens have experimented with hookah smoking. The Middle-Eastern tradition involves flavored tobacco, called shisha, which is often mixed with molasses and dried fruit. The shisha is burned in a water pipe, and the smoke is inhaled through a long hose. Hookahs are marketed as being safer than cigarettes, but they are not.[14] The smoke they produce contains nicotine, carbon monoxide, and other hazardous substances. Plus it can cause cancer just as other forms of smoking can.

The good news is that fewer U.S. kids are smoking. Only about five out of every hundred eighth-graders smoke regularly.[15] But each day, more than four thousand teens try their first cigarette, and another two thousand become daily smokers.[16] In fact, most smokers start by

An employee prepares a hookah for customers at a hookah lounge, where customers can pay to smoke flavored tobaccos.

age fifteen and are hooked by their eighteenth birthday.[17] Nicotine's highly addictive qualities keep many of them smoking for decades. Eventually, one out of three will die from smoking-related disease.[18]

Smokeless Tobacco

Chew and snuff are two types of smokeless tobacco. Chews are sold in a can or pouch in loose-leaf, twist, or plug forms. A person sucks on a plug, or wad, of it by placing it in his mouth between his cheek and gum. Snuff is finely ground tobacco that also comes in cans or pouches. Some people sniff it up their nose, while others use it much like chew or place it just inside their lower lip. Today, the most popular form of smokeless tobacco is moist snuff.[19]

Just as with smoking tobacco, chew and snuff contain formaldehyde, a fluid used to embalm dead bodies for burial. Both contain polonium 210, which are radioactive particles that turn into radon, and cadmium, a metallic element containing poisonous salts. When someone sticks chewing tobacco in their mouth, they are ingesting at least twenty-eight cancer-causing chemicals.[20] Holding that chew in the mouth for thirty minutes delivers as much nicotine as three cigarettes.[21] If they go through two cans of snuff per week, they will get as much nicotine as someone who smokes thirty cigarettes (a pack and a half) per day.[22]

Seventeen- to nineteen-year-old males use smokeless tobacco more than any other age group.[23] Most start by the ninth grade, while some begin using chew as early as the sixth grade.

This Associated Press photo shows a collection of chewing tobacco packages. During a news conference in 2001 in San Francisco, California, the Environmental Law Foundation announced a settlement against tobacco companies. Makers of chewing tobacco agreed to put warning signs on their products telling of the health hazards of smokeless tobacco.

Tobacco companies target kids by advertising at concerts and sports events.[24] Many kids who use chew or snuff may be imitating the rock stars and professional athletes they see using it.

Seventy percent of smokers and most smokeless tobacco users say they want to quit, and 35 percent try each year. But only 5 percent succeed.[25] Many of those who do not quit are among the more than 430,000 Americans who die each year as a result of tobacco use.[26] Cigarettes alone kill more Americans than alcohol, car accidents, suicide, AIDS, homicide, and illegal drugs combined.[27] Worldwide, the death toll from tobacco use is closer to 5 million.[28] For the tobacco industry, these numbers represent lost customers. To stay in business, tobacco companies must replace them.

CHAPTER TWO

NICOTINE'S JOURNEY

When a smoker puffs on a lit cigarette, he or she draws smoke into the mouth. The skin, gums, nose, and lining of the mouth absorb some nicotine. The remainder shoots straight down into the lungs, where it travels into the small blood vessels lining the lung walls. The blood vessels carry the nicotine to the heart, which then pumps it directly to the brain. All this takes about eight to ten seconds.[1] Nicotine from smoking reaches the brain even faster than it would if it were injected with a needle.[2]

Smokeless tobacco delivers a high dose of nicotine. Compared to a cigarette's 1.8-milligram dose, snuff has about 3.6 milligrams, and chew about 4.6 milligrams. But the level of nicotine in a person's blood throughout the day is about the same for both smokers and chew users.[3] Smokeless tobacco takes a bit longer to be absorbed into the blood stream through the gums. No matter how it gets in, when nicotine reaches the brain it excites millions of nerve cells. From there, nicotine is delivered to the rest of the body.

In the Brain

Our brains are made up of billions of nerve cells. They communicate by sending chemical messengers called neurotransmitters. Each neurotransmitter is like a key that fits into a special lock—called a receptor—located on the surface of nerve cells. Nicotine mimics the neurotransmitter called acetylcholine.[4] Depending on the region of the brain it is in, acetylcholine affects different areas of the body. It controls breathing, energy level, heartbeat, and other essential functions. Acetylcholine monitors how we process information in the brain and influences our learning and memory. It also sends signals to muscles.

Pretending to be acetylcholine, nicotine stimulates a burst of activity in some of these areas. For example, it makes a smoker feel more alert and increases his or her attention level. That is one reason people become addicted. Nicotine also acts as a depressant by interfering with the flow of information between nerve cells. As nicotine starts to leave a person's body, he or she becomes sluggish and needs more nicotine to function.

Nicotine also raises the levels of a neurotransmitter called dopamine.[5] Dopamine stimulates the areas of the brain that produce feelings of pleasure and reward. These areas involve appetite, learning, and memory. When a smoker inhales, nicotine causes a flood of dopamine in the

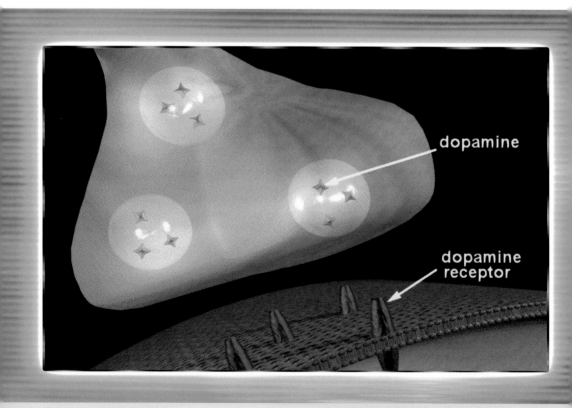

Nicotine raises the level of the neurotransmitter dopamine in the brain. The brain adjusts by cutting down on dopamine production.

brain. After repeated doses of nicotine, the brain changes. To adjust to too much dopamine, the brain cuts down on production. Then the smoker needs nicotine just to create normal levels of dopamine in the brain. Dopamine is the same neurotransmitter that is involved in addictions to other drugs, such as cocaine and heroin. Researchers now believe that this change in dopamine may play a key role in all addictions.[6] It may also explain why smokers have such a hard time quitting.

Making an Exit

Within ten to fifteen seconds of inhaling, most smokers feel nicotine's effects. Afterward, the drug does not stay long in the body. Though nicotine's effects occur mainly in the brain, the heart takes a hit as well. Studies have shown that a smoker's first cigarette of the day can increase the heart rate by ten to twenty beats a minute.[7] The amount of nicotine in the blood begins falling rapidly as soon as he or she stops smoking or chewing tobacco. The main byproduct of nicotine, cotinine, is widely used as in indicator in testing for exposure to nicotine. Enzymes in the liver break down about 80 percent into cotinine.[8] The lungs also process nicotine into cotinine and nicotine oxide. The body gets rid of some of these chemicals through urine. The rest is filtered from the blood through the kidneys and passed through urine.

Within forty-five minutes to a couple of hours, the concentration of nicotine in the blood is at about half of its peak.[9] As nicotine leaves—or is withdrawn from—the body, a person begins to feel withdrawal symptoms. For example, many smokers become edgy and depressed without a certain level of nicotine in their body. This is what drives them to smoke or chew throughout the day. They want to get that nicotine fix to keep feeling the drug's positive effects.

The time it takes to get rid of nicotine is different for each person. Some people have a gene that slows down the enzymes that break down nicotine in their liver.[10] After smoking, the nicotine levels in their blood and brain stay higher for a longer period of time. Normally, people keep smoking throughout the day to maintain a steady level of nicotine. But smokers with this gene end up smoking fewer cigarettes.

What's Your Poison?

About four thousand chemicals lurk in cigarettes and cigarette smoke. There are also several heavy metals—including lead, mercury, and nickel—that are especially damaging to our central nervous systems. Below is a small taste of some of the other toxic chemicals—along with common uses for them.[11]

Acetone:	**Nail polish remover**
Ammonia:	**Toilet cleaner**
Arsenic:	**Rat poison**
Benzene:	**Gasoline additive**
Butane:	**Gas grill fuel**
Cadmium:	**Batteries and oil paint**
Formaldehyde:	**Embalming fluid to preserve dead bodies**
Hydrogen cyanide:	**Gas chamber poison**
Styrene:	**Insulation material**
Toluene:	**Embalmers glue**
Turpentine:	**Paint thinner**

How Much Nicotine?

Over time, a tobacco user's brain becomes accustomed to a certain concentration of nicotine in the blood. This causes them to build a tolerance for the drug. Their brain actually tricks them into maintaining a set level of nicotine. Even smokers who switch to lower-nicotine cigarettes subconsciously smoke more cigarettes to get that level of nicotine. They inhale more deeply, hold the smoke longer, or cover the tiny holes in the filter.

Smokers do not know exactly how much nicotine is in their cigarettes. Tobacco companies are required by law to report nicotine levels to the Federal Trade Commission (FTC). But the way the companies measure those levels is flawed. The machine they use does not "inhale" smoke the way human beings do. In fact, a recent study found that smokers tend to inhale twice as much as the machine's chart.[12] For several years, public health officials and antismoking forces have been pushing to get tobacco regulated by the U.S. Food and Drug Administration (FDA).[13] In 2000, the U.S. Supreme Court ruled that the FDA does not have the right to regulate tobacco.[14] That pushed the regulation battle back to Congress. One of the issues is making measurement more accurate and in line with the way cigarettes are really used. Another is requiring tobacco companies to show more details about cigarette ingredients on the label. Without FDA regulation, the actual amount of nicotine in cigarettes will not likely match the level reported to the FTC.[15]

What About the Environment?

Smoking is a huge concern for the environment. Worldwide, 4.5 trillion cigarette butts are thrown on the ground each year.[16] That makes cigarettes a major source of litter. The cellulose acetate used to make cigarette filters can take decades to degrade in soil.[17] Meanwhile, cigarette butts release toxic chemicals into the soil and water.

MYTH		FACT
Smoking makes me look mature.	VS.	Smoking wrinkles your skin and stains your teeth before your time. There is nothing mature about smelling bad and inhaling lots of chemicals.

Cigarette butts are not only unsightly, they also release toxic chemicals into the soil and water.

That becomes a severe threat to plant and animal life. If an animal mistook the butts for food, they could block its digestive tract and cause it to starve to death.

Medical Use

Nicotine can stir up a lot of trouble. But it also may lead researchers to find better ways to treat diseases like Alzheimer's and schizophrenia.[18] Attention and memory, areas disrupted by these diseases, are stimulated by nicotine. Because nicotine is toxic, addictive, and becomes less effective with time, researchers are seeking a safe alternative. They are hoping to develop a drug that behaves similarly in the brain, without the dangerous side effects. Studies also need to determine the long-term effects of such a drug. Researchers agree that tobacco, with all of its harmful chemicals, is not a good or safe way to deliver nicotine.[19]

CHAPTER THREE

NICOTIANA: ONE PLANT'S STORY

The tobacco plant was first cultivated about seven thousand years ago in the Americas.[1] American Indians considered tobacco to be a sacred gift and used it in religious rituals. In the fifteenth century, American Indians greeted European explorers to their shores with gifts of tobacco.

By the mid-1500s, Spanish, Portuguese, and Dutch sailors were bringing tobacco to port cities around the world. Throughout Europe, doctors were using tobacco as medicine. They believed it could help treat toothaches, lockjaw, worms, and bad breath—even cancer and other serious illnesses. As early as 1602, however, a link was drawn between the lung diseases suffered by chimney sweeps (caused by soot) and illnesses that might have been caused by tobacco.[2]

In many countries, tobacco use was not tolerated. In 1634, Czar Alexis of Russia created new penalties for smoking. For the first offense, the punishment was whipping, a slit nose, and being sent to Siberia. The punishment for the second offense was execution.[3] At the same time, anyone caught using or selling tobacco in China faced decapitation. By the 1650s, however, snuff had become popular throughout China and remained so until the early twentieth century.[4]

In the mid-1700s, Swedish botanist Carolus Linnaeus named the tobacco plant genus, *Nicotiana*.[5] He named it after Nicot de Villemain, an ambassador who introduced the plant to France in the mid-sixteenth century. Linnaeus also

Swedish botanist Carolus Linnaeus named the tobacco plant genus, *Nicotiana*, in the 18th century.

described two species of *Nicotiana*. One, *Nicotiana rustica*, was the somewhat bitter tobacco native to the American colonies. The other, *Nicotiana tabacum*, was a sweet and mild tobacco that John Rolfe, founder of Virginia tobacco and husband to Pocohantas, had transplanted from the Spanish West Indies in 1611.[6]

The American Colonies

In the colonies, tobacco had great value. It was used as money throughout the seventeenth and eighteenth centuries. But the booming crop also led to slavery. In 1619, the first ship carrying slaves arrived from Africa.[7] The workers were baptized as Christians, which meant they could not be enslaved for life. They were supposed to be indentured servants, just like many of the English colonists, who would work for a certain number of years in exchange for food and shelter. Some received a small wage.

Over time, however, things changed. Plantation owners needed more workers for the labor-intensive crop and were not willing to let go of the servants they had. More ships arrived from Africa, and before long the success of tobacco

Tobacco was so valuable during the seventeenth and eighteenth centuries that it was used as currency.

made slavery commonplace. In 1705, the Virginia Assembly passed a law legalizing lifelong slavery.[8]

Tobacco growers became deeply indebted to British merchants who sold their product. By 1776, they owed millions of pounds.[9] Colonists were also tired of paying taxes on their harvest to the English government. With talk of rebellion brewing, Benjamin Franklin turned to France for a loan to finance the American Revolution. He got it by promising 5 million pounds of Virginia tobacco.[10] When the war ended in 1783, America had won its independence from England. It then used its own tax on tobacco to help repay the war debt.

The Nineteenth Century

In the early 1800s, most tobacco factories made chewing tobacco. But cigars gained popularity in the north following the Mexican War (1846–1848), when soldiers returned with Latin American cigars. In London, England, Philip Morris opened a tobacco shop selling hand-rolled Turkish cigarettes. His business grew to become the international Philip Morris tobacco company; today, it is called Altria Group.

During the Civil War (1861–1865), soldiers were given tobacco with their food rations. To help pay for the war, the federal government taxed tobacco.[11] Just before the Civil War started, 350,000 slaves had been working the tobacco plantations.[12] With the end of the war came freedom for all of them. Slavery was abolished.

Despite centuries of tobacco use, very little was known about the science of tobacco or its health effects. The first report of nicotine's effects on the brain came out in 1889.[13] Scientists suggested that the brain has receptors and transmitters that are stimulated by specific chemicals.

These miniature bottles from the late 1700s contained the finely ground tobacco powder, or snuff, that was snorted by people from all walks of life.

It was a groundbreaking idea that proved to be correct.

The Early Twentieth Century

By 1901, forty-three of the forty-five states had established anticigarette laws and were considering passing even tougher restrictions.[14] In 1903, Kansas enacted the "slobbering" bill, which banned the spitting of tobacco in churches, schools, and public buildings. A movement was also in the works to get tobacco included in the Federal Food and Drugs Act of 1906. The act prohibited the sale of certain foods and drugs and required honest statement of contents on labels. Though nicotine was originally on the list, lobbyists from the tobacco industry managed to get it removed. They argued that it was not a drug because it was not used to cure or prevent disease.

Despite these efforts, World War I (1914–1918) led to an explosion of nicotine addicts. Soldiers were provided with all the free cigarettes they could smoke. After the war, cigarette consumption and lung cancer rates continued to grow hand-in-hand.[15]

In 1950, a persuasive study connecting smoking and lung cancer was published in the *Journal of the*

Many years ago, advertisements for cigarettes were more common than they are today.

American Medical Association.[16] A study in the same issue found that 96.5 percent of lung cancer patients interviewed were moderately heavy- to chain-smokers. Smoking continually, chain-smokers often light the next cigarette soon after their previous one.

Tobacco Industry

As more research came out about the health hazards of cigarettes, the major tobacco companies fought back. They formed two public relations firms: one came to be called the Council for Tobacco Research, and the other the Tobacco Institute (TI). They published booklets and ran advertisements claiming that smoking was safe.[17]

Tobacco companies continued to deny publicly any links between their products and cancer or other diseases. They also denied that nicotine is addictive. However, decades later, internal documents were released that proved the industry knew otherwise. Tobacco company Brown & Williamson's general counsel wrote in 1963, ". . . nicotine is addictive. We are, then, in the business of selling nicotine, an addictive drug effective in the release of stress mechanisms."[18]

What comes in this box,

Also comes in this box.

Cyanide is the deadly ingredient in rat poison.
And just one of the many in cigarettes.

Mounting Evidence

In 1965, Congress passed the Federal Cigarette Labeling and Advertising Act. It required each cigarette pack to carry a warning on its label.[19] Two years later, a surgeon general's report concluded that smoking is the principal cause of lung cancer, and found evidence linking smoking to heart disease. By 1969, Congress strengthened the cigarette labeling law so each pack had to read, "Warning: The Surgeon General Has Determined That Cigarette Smoking Is Dangerous to Your Health."[20] However, the law also gave tobacco companies an out against other legal action. As long as tobacco ads and packaging carried the surgeon general's warning, the companies were protected from state regulations.

By the early 1970s, a movement to protect nonsmokers' rights was gaining momentum. Nonsmokers were protesting the clouds of cigarette smoke that filled public spaces. The airline industry responded by creating nonsmoking sections. As it became clear that cigarette and cigar smoke harmed nonsmokers, too, other measures were passed. The 1975 Minnesota Clean Indoor Air Act prohibited smoking in public places, except in designated smoking areas.[21] It was the first law to require separation of smokers and nonsmokers. The Tobacco Institute reported in 1978 that the nonsmokers' rights movement was the most dangerous development that the tobacco industry had yet faced.[22] In response, it launched an advertising campaign against the movement.

Growing evidence of tobacco's dangers brought about more regulations to protect users and nonusers. In 1986, a U.S. surgeon general's report focused on secondhand smoke, but also declared that smokeless tobacco is addictive and causes cancer. The 1988 surgeon general's report spotlighted nicotine and its effects on the body, stating that cigarettes and other forms of tobacco are addicting because of nicotine.[23] The Winter Olympics, held that year in Calgary, Alberta, took notice and banned smoking.

The 1990s

In 1993, the U.S. Environmental Protection Agency declared cigarette smoke a Class-A carcinogen. This means it is a pollutant that has been shown to cause cancer in people. As a result, the mid-1990s saw a number of new regulations and lawsuits. Once again, the FDA sought the right to regulate tobacco and its advertising. The largest tobacco companies and the advertising industry immediately filed suit against the FDA proposal.

In 1994, tobacco industry CEOs testified before Congress that they did not believe cigarettes were addictive or caused cancer. A month later, a large number of internal industry documents were leaked to the University of California and various news media. They revealed that tobacco companies had known for decades about the serious dangers of tobacco and nicotine.[24] Tobacco scientists and researchers began testifying before Congress that their employers had covered up their research linking nicotine to addiction and disease.

Beginning in 1996, Liggett Tobacco became the first company to settle one lawsuit after another. As a result, the company was required to issue a public statement acknowledging that "as the Surgeon General and respected medical researchers have found, cigarette smoking causes health problems, including lung cancer, heart and vascular disease and emphysema. . . . Liggett acknowledges that the tobacco industry markets to youth, which means those fewer than eighteen

During the 1990s, tobacco companies were forced to acknowledge the harm caused by their products.

years of age . . . Liggett condemns this practice and will not market to children."[25]

The major tobacco companies proposed a way to settle all the lawsuits at once. Ultimately, the U.S. Senate rejected the proposed settlement, because it was not tough enough. Individuals, states, insurers, and others went forward with lawsuits against tobacco companies. They wanted to be compensated for tobacco-related pain, suffering, and medical costs.

In 1998, forty-six states finally reached an agreement with tobacco companies to settle lawsuits. (Four states had already settled lawsuits by 1998.)[26] The Master Settlement Agreement required companies to pay for antismoking campaigns and banned them from targeting kids with their advertising. They could not sell their products through vending machines, outdoor advertising, or by sponsoring sports events where kids might be. The Tobacco Institute and other tobacco-funded groups were shut down. Over the next few years, forty-eight states received funds for tobacco prevention and control programs.[27]

The Twenty-First Century

So far, this century has seen higher cigarette taxes and expanded smoking bans. Lawsuits against tobacco companies continued across the country, and the companies were ordered to pay out billions of dollars to individuals and insurance companies. As a judge for a 2001 trial charged, "Philip Morris knew by the late 1950s and early 1960s that the nicotine in cigarettes is highly addictive, that substances in cigarette tar cause lung cancer, and that no substantial medical or scientific doubt existed on these crucial facts."[28] The

Smoking Bans

Over the past four decades, public health initiatives and the nonsmokers' movement have led to a succession of restrictions on tobacco use. States and local communities have progressively banned smoking in public spaces and work sites. The following extended such bans across national and international borders.

1971   Cigarette advertising is banned on radio and television.[30]

1988   Smoking is banned on U.S. flights less than two hours.[31]
       Smoking is banned from Olympic Games.

1990   Smoking is banned on interstate buses and U.S. flights less than six hours.[32]

1993   Tobacco is banned throughout minor-league baseball.[33]

2000   Smoking ban is extended to all U.S. international flights.[34]

2002   Ban on smoking takes effect throughout the U.S. military.[35]

judge went on to criticize tobacco companies for their greed, deception, and targeting of underage smokers.

In 1999, the U.S. Department of Justice filed a lawsuit against major tobacco companies.[29] The government has demanded $289 billion for the fifty-plus years that the companies defrauded the public through illegal and dangerous practices. The trial finally began in September 2004.

A growing awareness about the dangers of nicotine and tobacco has led to changes around the world. Smoking bans have been enforced or strengthened in public places throughout Europe and the Americas. The European Union now requires tougher, more visible health warnings on cigarette packs. Tobacco advertising has been restricted in parts of Europe and Asia.

Unfortunately, many poor countries still lack

MYTH		FACT
I can smoke if I want to.	VS.	Smoking is not about being independent. It is addictive, and being an addict makes you more dependent than independent.

regulations against dishonest advertising. Half of the 5 million people who die each year from tobacco-caused diseases are in developing countries.[36] But the World Health Organization has been working to correct that with the Framework Convention on Tobacco Control.[37]

This global health treaty became law in 2005. It requires member countries to take measures to reduce tobacco use, such as banning certain tobacco advertising and restricting sales. For example, many countries print large graphic warnings on cigarette packages, others have outlawed cigarette vending machines and banned advertising in newspapers, magazines, and on television. As of early 2006, signers of the treaty represent 113 countries and 74 percent of the world's population. If they meet their goal, they hope to reduce tobacco use by at least 50 percent and save 200 million lives by the year 2050.

CHAPTER FOUR

BODY OF EVIDENCE

"I was at an autopsy last week . . . we thought it might be a homicide victim," reports Detective Sandra Oplinger of the San Diego, California, Police Department.[1] "In the end, it was determined to be an accident involving several drugs and a gashed foot. But what caught my eye," notes Oplinger, "was the woman's lungs. They were so spotted from her smoking that they looked like someone had thrown hot ashes all over them. And she was only 25 years old!"[2]

Dr. William Doyle has seen a lot of lung cancer in his forty-plus years as a pathologist in New England.[3] A pathologist is a doctor who studies diseases. One of the pathologist's responsibilities is performing autopsies to determine how a person died.

"Normal lungs are whitish pink," says Doyle. "But carbon from tobacco, car exhaust, and other pollutants turns the lungs ashen-gray to black."[4] Though other factors (such as radioactive gas, asbestos, and family history) can increase someone's risk of lung cancer, smoking tobacco is the major risk factor.[5] It is estimated that smokers are ten to twenty times more likely to develop lung cancer than nonsmokers. The tumors that typically develop, explains Doyle, form "round masses that could be the size of a golf ball or a tennis ball. They're blackish, with a fleshy look. Over time, the mass hardens. As tumors get bigger, they outgrow their blood supply."[6] If parts metastasize, or break away and travel to the brain and other organs, Doyle notes, "that usually spells death."

Smoking does not always cause lung cancer, and the lungs are not the only part of the body affected by tobacco. Snuff and chew, especially, can lead to cancers of the mouth and throat.

Sean's Case

"I'm afraid we'll have to remove that part of the tongue, Sean," said the throat specialist.[7] The high school senior was silent.[8]

Sean had been using chew and snuff since he was twelve years old. He went through a can of snuff every day and a half. Aside from his addiction to nicotine, he led a healthy life. Boasting twenty-eight track medals, Sean had been voted his high school's most outstanding athlete.[9]

Then, one day, Sean noticed an ugly red sore on his tongue. It was about the size of a half-dollar with a hard white core. He went in for surgery a few weeks later. The doctor had to remove more of Sean's tongue than anticipated. Even worse, the biopsy came back positive—Sean had cancer. He would have to be treated with radiation therapy. Just before starting therapy, however, a swollen lymph node was found on Sean's neck. The cancer had spread. Sean now needed to have neck surgery.

This time, the doctor removed lymph nodes, muscle, and blood vessels. Sean now had a huge scar that ran from his earlobe to his breastbone. But after five weeks of radiation and healing, Sean seemed to be doing well.[10]

Then, a few months later, a CAT scan showed a cancerous thread down his back and near the base of his brain. Sean went in for a third operation. This time, they had to remove his lower jaw on the right side.

Within two months, Sean found two new lumps in his left cheek. One day Sean admitted to his mother that he still craved snuff. "I catch myself thinking," he said, "I'll just reach over and have a dip."[11]

MYTH		FACT
Chew is safer than smoking.	vs.	Tobacco is tobacco. The nicotine still gets you hooked, and the chemicals are just as toxic.

Less than a year after finding the sore, Sean died. He was nineteen years old.

Though most chew or snuff users do not suffer such a tragic experience, Sean's case shows how addictive nicotine can be. It does not always lead to cancer, but adolescents who use smokeless tobacco are more likely to become cigarette smokers.[12] The combination can increase their risk of cancer and other diseases.

The Killers

Cancers account for fewer than half of the deaths related to smoking.[13] Tobacco kills even more people through heart disease and stroke than it does through cancer.[14] Nicotine shrinks the blood vessels, which slows down blood flow and stresses the heart.

"Cigarette smoking speeds up heart disease," notes Doyle. "The arteries clog up with fatty deposits that look like yellowed toothpaste. Eventually, they harden and the heart starves, because it's not getting any nutrients."[15] Nicotine does so much damage to arteries that many surgeons refuse to operate on patients with artery disease, unless they stop smoking.

When nicotine hits a person's system, it releases

adrenaline, which increases heart rate and blood pressure. The heart then needs more oxygen to handle the workload, but its oxygen supply does not increase. It must do extra work with no extra help. Besides nicotine, the most dangerous chemicals in cigarette smoke are carbon monoxide and tar.[16]

The carbon monoxide is what leads to heart problems and strokes. Carbon monoxide causes those cholesterol deposits to develop in artery walls. It makes the heart beat faster and blood clot more easily. Carbon monoxide also robs the blood of oxygen. All these stresses damage and weaken a smoker's heart and increase the risk of heart attack.[17] People sometimes get dizzy and sick to the stomach from smoking, especially the first time. That is caused by the carbon monoxide and lack of oxygen exchange in their lungs.

Tar is what causes lung cancer, bronchial diseases, and emphysema. With chronic bronchitis, the airways produce excess mucus, which forces a smoker to cough more often. Emphysema slowly destroys a person's ability to breathe. In later stages of the disease, people need help breathing with an oxygen bottle or through oxygen

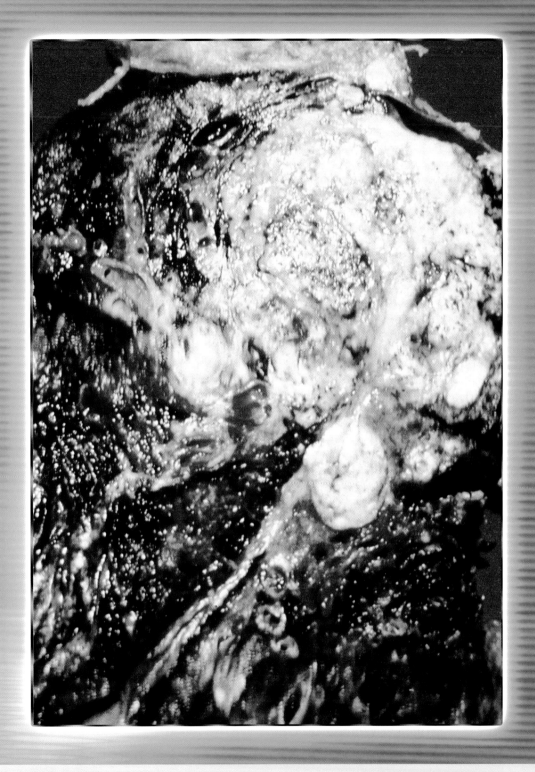

This is the cross section of a human lung of someone who died from cancer. The white area in the upper lobe is cancer, and the black areas indicate that the person was a smoker.

tubes in the nose. When a person suffers from both chronic bronchitis and emphysema, it is called chronic obstructive pulmonary disease (COPD).[18] COPD makes a person gasp for breath all the time—as if he or she were drowning.

Other chemicals in tobacco may cause the diseases, but nicotine is the reason a person keeps smoking or chewing. Nicotine alone is an extremely toxic poison. A drop of pure nicotine would kill a person.[19] In fact, nicotine is deadly enough that it is used as a pesticide on crops.

Smoking Tobacco

In the brain, nicotine makes a smoker feel more alert. But at the same time, it calms the person. Researchers are not certain whether that calming effect is from the nicotine or simply from an addicted person satisfying a craving. As a person's nervous system adapts to nicotine, he or she needs more tobacco to feel the same perkiness. The more he or she smokes or chews, the more nicotine he or she will have in the blood. Eventually, the smoker will level off and have to maintain that nicotine amount.[20] Otherwise the smoker will go through withdrawal.

Some people say they smoke because it

suppresses their appetite. They do not want to quit because they fear they will gain weight. The problem is that staying thin this way is temporary and unhealthy. It may be that they do not have much of an appetite, because smoking dulls their sense of smell and taste. If they cannot taste food,

Smoking while pregnant is not only harmful to the smoker, but also very damaging to the unborn child.

they are less likely to eat. A steady diet of smoking, however, will also weaken their lungs. That means they will have less stamina for exercise and sports. Over time, smokers can develop thinner skin and what some people call smoker's face.[21] A lack of oxygen to the skin causes an unhealthy grayish tone and more wrinkles.

Even more immediate effects of tobacco are bad breath and yellow teeth. Eventually the teeth may turn black. Tobacco also rots the teeth and causes gum disease. Simply being around a smoker can make someone's hair and clothes stink. Smoking can also cause diarrhea. The increased acid in the stomach can lead to ulcers.[22]

Though almost all cigarette smokers inhale, many cigar smokers do not. How much nicotine gets absorbed through cigars depends on how a person smokes. Some people stick a cigar in their mouth and leave it there until the end is soggy. They will absorb much more nicotine than those who mostly hold the cigar and puff now and then. To make cigars easier to inhale, some cigar companies have changed their curing and fermenting process. That same process adds more harmful ingredients to a smoker's body.

Smoke from cigars and cigarettes contain many of the same toxic compounds. No matter how someone smokes a cigar, they expose their lips, mouth, and throat to cancer-causing chemicals. This makes their risk of oral cancer similar to that of cigarette smokers.[23] Smokers who do not inhale cigars may have a lower risk of lung cancer or heart disease than do cigarette smokers. But they are still putting themselves in danger. Those who do inhale are eleven times more likely than nonsmokers to die from lung cancer.[24]

Smokeless Tobacco

Watch almost any baseball game and you will see some of the players chewing tobacco. No evidence shows that tobacco helps physical reaction time or power of movement. But there are studies that show nicotine actually decreases the speed and force of leg movements during reaction-time tests.[25] That is on top of the stress it places on a person's heart.

Chew and snuff stain a person's teeth and cause bad breath. Some people have a problem with cracked lips and bleeding in their mouth. They could get gum disease. That makes the gums draw back and exposes tooth roots, which

A 27-year-old cancer survivor discusses his experiences with chewing tobacco, cancer, doctors, and disfiguring surgeries during an anti-tobacco assembly.

makes a person's teeth very sensitive to pain and open to other disease. Sugar from smokeless tobacco mixed with the plaque on teeth forms acids that eat away at tooth enamel, which causes cavities. Studies have shown that about one-quarter of the people who regularly use smokeless tobacco have receding gums and bone loss around the teeth.[26] A person slowly gets rid of the chew or snuff by spitting it out. But he or she will end up swallowing some of it, too. Because of this, the nicotine in smokeless tobacco can also lead to cancer of the stomach and digestive tract.

Nearly 60 percent of the people who use smokeless tobacco develop leukoplakia, a condition in which leathery white patches form on the gums, tongue, and inside the cheek.[27] The patches can show up within a few months of starting snuff or chew. A small percentage of leukoplakic patches can become cancerous, and many cancers of the mouth occur next to the patches.[28] The sores typically appear at the spots in the mouth where a person places the chew. One study found that nearly 75 percent of daily snuff and chew users had sores in their mouths.[29] The longer a person uses smokeless tobacco, the more likely he or she is to get leukoplakia.

The most serious risk with smokeless tobacco is oral cancer.[30] Cancers of the mouth and throat are the most common. Surgery to remove oral cancers can mean disfiguring changes to the face. Or worse, the cancer could spread. Snuff users develop oral cancer several times more frequently than do people who do not use tobacco. For long-time snuff users, the risk of cheek and gum cancer may increase nearly fifty times.[31]

Secondhand Smoke

When people who do not smoke are exposed to secondhand smoke, it is called involuntary smoking or passive smoking. That is because, without bringing a cigarette to their lips, they absorb the same nicotine and harmful chemicals that smokers do. The more secondhand smoke a person is exposed to, the greater the harm to the body.

Secondhand smoke is a mixture of two forms of smoke: sidestream smoke and mainstream smoke. Sidestream smoke is what comes off the end of a lighted cigarette, pipe, or cigar. Mainstream smoke is what is exhaled by a smoker.[32] Sidestream smoke has a higher concentration of cancer-causing chemicals than either mainstream smoke or the smoke that a smoker inhales through a cigarette filter.[33] In 1986, the surgeon general issued the first report on passive smoking. The report said passive smoking causes disease, including lung cancer, in healthy nonsmokers. It also stated that children of parents who smoke had greater respiratory problems than did children of nonsmoking parents.

Since that report came out, evidence has piled up showing that secondhand smoke causes disease in healthy nonsmokers. In the United States alone, passive smoking kills about three thousand nonsmokers each year with lung cancer.[34] Another 35,000 to 40,000 die each year from heart disease.[35] Respiratory infections, such as pneumonia and bronchitis, afflict 150,000 to

Smoking at an early age can cause many health problems.

Self-Restoration

The sooner a smoker quits, the more he or she can reduce the chances of getting cancer and other diseases.[36] Smoking directly damages the respiratory system; quitting can help repair but not completely reverse that.[37] To what extent the body can restore itself depends on when the person started smoking, how long he or she smoked, and how much was inhaled.

- Within 20 minutes of quitting: The heart rate drops.

- 12 hours later: The carbon monoxide level in blood drops to normal.

- 2 weeks to 3 months later: Circulation improves and lung function increases.

- 1 to 9 months later: Coughing and shortness of breath decrease; cilia (tiny hairlike structures on the surface of cells) regain normal function to clean the lungs and reduce the risk of infection.

- 1 year later: The excess risk of heart disease is half that of a smoker's.

- 5 to 15 years later: Risk of stroke is gradually reduced.

- 10 years later: The lung cancer death rate is about half that of a continuing smoker's. The risk of cancer of the mouth, throat, and esophagus decreases.

- 15 years later: The risk of heart disease is reduced, closer to that of a nonsmoker's.

300,000 children younger than eighteen months old. Nearly one million children annually suffer severe asthma attacks more frequently due to passive smoke.[38] Other respiratory problems endured by nonsmokers include coughing, phlegm, chest discomfort, and weakened lungs. Passive smoking also appears to influence a child's decision to smoke, which may be because he or she is imitating a parent's smoking habit, has been affected by exposure to addictive nicotine, or has easier access to cigarettes. A child is likely influenced by some combination of all three. The majority (75 percent) of teenagers who smoke have parents who smoke.[39]

CHAPTER FIVE

THE ANTI-SOCIAL

Glenn Wagner, chief pathologist at the San Diego County Medical Examiner's Office, has been dealing with death and how it happens for decades.[1] Whether someone dies from cancer, an accident, or something else, he says, "Most cases I see are people who have made a bad decision at a bad time in a bad way. Smoking is usually not the only cause of death," comments Wagner. "But, in my experience, those who smoke are likely to engage in other risky behavior."[2]

Truth or Consequences

Remember the teens from Chapter 1 who were parked on the side of the road? After Officer Wheeler got back to the police station, he followed up on their stories with some phone calls.[3]

"When I talked to the friend they were supposedly going to see, he was surprised and didn't know what to say. I asked him if it was true, if his friends were coming over to his house. At first, he said, 'Yeah, okay.' But then he tried to backpedal and said, 'Well, my parents don't really want me to have friends over.'"[4] There were never any plans for his friends to come over to play video games.

What about the fifteen-year-old who was arrested for underage possession of tobacco? Wheeler reports, "In court, he will likely get probation and pay about $150 in probation costs. State law requires that he also go to eight hours of tobacco education class."[5]

Probation typically includes about fifty hours of

community service. That could be anything from painting over graffiti and picking up trash to moving furniture and power-washing walkways. According to the Texas by-laws, both the class and community service are not meant as punishment. They are intended to be an education about the dangers of smoking.

Punishment may not be the main reason. But, as Wheeler points out, "No kid wants to spend

There are eight states in which minors who are repeatedly arrested for buying or possessing tobacco can potentially lose their drivers licenses.

his free time picking up trash. And he especially doesn't want his friends seeing him do it."[6]

Minnesota, Vermont, and Oklahoma are among the eight states that might also take away the drivers license of minors who are repeatedly arrested for buying or possessing tobacco. Fifteen states—including Florida, Washington, and Maryland—may require minors to attend smoking education classes, as well as pay fines.[7]

If they buy tobacco underage, it is not just the teens who suffer consequences. In most areas, store clerks and owners who sell cigarettes to someone under the state's legal age (age eighteen in every state, except Alaska, Alabama, and Utah where it is nineteen) face hundreds of dollars in fines. The store could also have its license to sell tobacco suspended for a few months—or lose that license altogether.

Smoking Tobacco

Most kids get their cigarettes from friends or family members. According to the *American Journal of Preventive Medicine*, about 65 percent of kids who smoke said they have friends or relatives buy them cigarettes.[8] About half of the students said they bought cigarettes themselves from a local convenience store or gas station. Few of them had to provide proof of age, even though all fifty states and the District of Columbia restrict tobacco sales to minors.

"The best news is that smoking among kids is down and quite dramatically," says one researcher.[9] Higher cigarette prices are probably the main reason there has been a drop in teen smoking. Attitudes toward smoking are another. More and more kids understand that smoking is dangerous and that their peers find it unattractive. In a recent survey of teens, about three-quarters of high school seniors said they prefer to date someone who does not smoke.[10]

Social smokers claim to only smoke in social situations, such as at parties—but it does not take much to develop a chemical dependence. They may already be addicted long before they realize it. Kids who smoke regularly are already addicted to nicotine and experience the same addiction as adult smokers. Only three out of every hundred high school smokers think they will be smoking in five years. But in reality, studies show that three out of five will still be smoking eight years later.[11]

MYTH	FACT
I can smoke or dip for a few years without getting cancer. vs.	It is not just long-term users who risk disease. People who have used tobacco for as few as six years have gotten cancer.

Smokeless Tobacco

Smokeless tobacco does not have the smoke that most people find offensive. But chewing and dipping are socially unappealing, especially to the opposite sex. Both methods cause excess saliva, which makes a person drool. As with cigarettes and cigars, bad breath and discolored teeth are not only ugly, they are also embarrassing. Chew and snuff users get rid of most of the tobacco in their mouth by spitting.

One study that surveys eighth-, tenth-, and twelfth-graders across the country found that, as of 1995, students increasingly have been turned off by smokeless tobacco. This is not solely because of social reasons, but also because the risks of mouth and throat cancer have become increasingly well known.[12]

Secondhand Smoke

Without even touching a cigarette, people near a smoker may get watery eyes and headaches from secondhand smoke. That smoke also carries toxic chemicals that are just as deadly for those around it as for those who smoke. Secondhand smoke is the third leading cause of preventable death in the United States (after smoking and drug abuse).[13] By sitting in the presence of smoke for only minutes, a nonsmoker's primary artery that carries blood from the heart to the rest of the body stiffens as much as it does for a smoker who smokes one cigarette.[14]

Children exposed to passive smoking are also likely to do worse at school than their peers. A study of nearly 4,400 children between six and sixteen years old was conducted by the U.S. Children's Environmental Health Center.[15] It found that exposure to even low levels of tobacco smoke in the home was linked to lower test results for reading and math. Whether the exposure took place in the womb or after being born was difficult to determine. The authors recommended future studies to address the issue. This study confirmed that the greater the exposure to passive smoke, the worse the child's decline was.

It Costs How Much?

The serious health and social aspects are not even the only problem. The tobacco habit can be expensive. With a pack of cigarettes costing any-where from $4 to $8, a person can spend a lot of money on tobacco. A pack-a-day smoker, for example, might spend $6 a day. That may not seem like much, but it adds up to $2,190 per year. At 20 cigarettes per pack, that means smoking 7,300 cigarettes per year. Over a decade, that is $21,900. That money could buy a lot of CDs, new clothes, a car, and more.

The cost in time is also significant. The same pack-a-day smokers who average ten minutes per cigarette spend about three hours and twenty minutes a day on the habit. In a year, they will spend 1,205 hours. By the end of a decade, they will have dedicated 12,050 hours to smoking.

Knowledge Is Power

In the 1998 Master Settlement Agreement, tobacco companies vowed to stop marketing to children under the age of eighteen. But they still

Another antismoking ad from the U.S. Department of Health and Human Services suggests that women do not want to date smokers.

advertise in youth-oriented magazines. And they continue to advertise heavily at stores near schools and playgrounds. The Massachusetts Department of Health ran a study of tobacco advertising in magazines read by a lot of kids.[16] The study revealed that in the year after the settlement cigarette advertising actually increased by 33 percent. A study in the *New England Journal of Medicine* found that tobacco companies spent $59.6 million for advertising in the most popular magazines among kids in 2000.[17]

Flavors are another trick. To hook first-timers on a product that does not taste very good, tobacco companies add sugar and sweet flavorings.

Though studies have proven over and over that nicotine is a drug, tobacco is still not regulated by the U.S. Food and Drug Administration (FDA). Money has a lot to do with that. In October 2004, a majority of a Senate committee voted for FDA authority over tobacco products. But a majority of a House committee voted against it. Those who voted against FDA regulation had received a lot more money from the tobacco industry. From 1999 to 2004, they had received, on average, nearly five times more money than those who voted *for* FDA regulation.[18]

FDA regulation may not be important to some kids. But many simply do not like being lied to. Across the country, they have organized to get the truth out about tobacco. These are teens working with teens. Some take part in programs, such as Teens Against Tobacco Use (TATU, sponsored by the American Lung Association), that train high school students to work with middle and elementary school students. The American Legacy Foundation, which was established as a result of the 1998 tobacco settlement, provides Web sites—complete with message boards, scientific information, and stories from real teens that have made changes in their community. These sites not only educate, but help youth make their voices heard. Several states have organizations that do similar work.

CHAPTER SIX

TAKE CHARGE

"I don't need to smoke; I can quit anytime." "Cigarettes are way too easy to get."[1] These are the sort of comments social worker Molly Gallegos and guidance counselor Carla Herried often hear. The two women help teens quit smoking through the American Lung Association's Not On Tobacco (NOT) program.

"They hear and read that minors can't buy tobacco," says Gallegos. "But they know they can get them at the gas station down the street. They're angry about that. They don't think it's right."[2]

In a Wisconsin suburb, Gallegos and Herried work with groups of five or six teens who meet once a week for eight weeks. Boys meet in one group, girls in another. They discuss why they want to quit smoking, and share stories of how they got started. The counselors help them learn to deal with their cravings, withdrawal symptoms, and social issues. They teach them about healthy alternatives to smoking. The teens can keep journals, if they want, to help them understand and overcome the reasons they smoke.

"About 95 percent of the kids in our program have parents or siblings who smoke," reports Gallegos. "It's hard for them to quit when they're surrounded by people who smoke."[3]

So how does someone avoid addiction? "In the course of the program," says Herried, "we ask teens what they would tell younger kids about smoking. Easy, they say: Don't start."[4]

Once addicted, trying to quit is not easy. The

Top Ten Reasons Not to Use Tobacco

There are endless reasons not to smoke or dip. But if you are thinking about it, consider these ten first. If someone else is pushing you to try it, try simply saying "no thanks." You do not have to justify that response to anyone. But if they persist, tell them you do not want to use tobacco because:

1. It pollutes your body.

2. You do not want to be controlled by addiction.

3. It tastes gross.

4. You can save money for better things.

5. You do not want to smell like an ashtray.

6. How about those yellow teeth?

7. You are allergic to smoke.

8. It turns most people off.

9. Chew and snuff make you drool.

10. You are on a smoke-free diet.

lack of nicotine is uncomfortable. It makes a person cranky and irritable. Some people get hostile and aggressive when they try to quit. This is because their brain has not yet recovered. It needs a little more time to get used to the body's natural chemicals again.

Withdrawal

Gallegos and Herried give their teens rewards for making it through each week tobacco free. They might get candy, a CD case, a small toy, or other fun stuff.

"For Quit Day in session five, we throw a pizza party," says Herried. "We give the kids a small bag with mints, mouthwash, air-freshener for the car, incentives to keep their minds off of smoking; Silly Putty gives their hands something to do instead of holding a cigarette."[5]

Gallegos adds, "This is when reality begins to set in. They have been talking about quitting for four weeks, but now they actually have to do it."[6]

"The first couple of weeks after quitting, they discuss how and when they turned down cigarettes," says Gallegos.[7] Students often point to the period just before and after school as particularly tempting. If their friends light up, it is hard to

Many teens do not smoke and find activities and clubs that promote their healthy lifestyle.

resist. For those whose parents or siblings smoke, home can also be a challenge.

"They also talk about their physical symptoms," notes Gallegos. "The stomachaches, being tired, coughing up phlegm. The group atmosphere helps them get through it."[8] During one session, a student shared his experience in drug and alcohol rehabilitation. He told the group how addicted he had been, that it was so bad he had to be admitted to the hospital. He was off the other drugs, but now he was trying to quit smoking, too. It helped the rest of the group understand how controlling any drug can be.

After eight weeks, the kids have been through a lot together. They have met a challenge and have tried to help each other overcome it. "By the last session," notes Gallegos, "they're very excited about their accomplishment. But they're also scared, because now they have to do it on their own."[9]

"Some kids come back for a pep talk a few weeks after the program ends," adds Herried. "They may have relapsed and had a cigarette. Sometimes, they just want to talk about a problem they're having with a friend or at home that made them want to smoke."[10]

A lot of people who quit also get depressed without that regular jolt of nicotine. As their body adjusts, they tend to feel tired and restless. The first few days after quitting are usually the worst. But most people say that after about two weeks, it gets better. It can be months before the cravings are mostly gone.

At the same time, trying to stay off tobacco means resisting all the triggers that make a person want another cigarette or chew or snuff. That is

Help a Friend Quit

If you know someone who wants to quit, you can help by being part of his or her support group. Quitting is not easy, so be patient. And be prepared for the mood swings and crankiness. Here are ways you can help.

1. Make a list of the reasons why he or she wants to quit. They can refer back to this list when temptation strikes.

2. Stock up on oral substitutes—sunflower seeds, sugarless gum, carrot sticks, beef jerky, cinnamon sticks, hard candy.

3. Decide on a plan: Should he or she quit cold turkey, use Nicotine Replacement Therapy, attend a class?

4. Make a list of triggers, which can be situations, places, or emotions that make him or her want to light up or dip. Being aware of these can help him or her avoid them.

5. When cravings do strike, encourage him or her to take a few calming deep breaths, chew gum, or exercise. Drinking more water will help to flush out the chemicals.

6. Help him or her find a new, healthy habit to replace smoking or using chew.

7. Let him or her know you are there if he or she wants to share thoughts and feelings about their struggle.

the psychological withdrawal. Hanging out with friends who smoke is one trigger. Working with people who smoke on their breaks could be another. For athletes who use chew or snuff, going to practice might be a frequent trigger. Confronting these triggers is probably the best way to beat them.

As one ex-smoker put it, "I decided to do each thing ten times without a cigarette. I'd get in the car, drive to the store, and crave a cigarette all the way there. But each time I didn't light up, the urge was less and less. Honestly, it was six months before I felt comfortable without a cigarette in my hand."[11]

People can have strong desires to use tobacco months or even years after they quit. It might hit them when they least expect it. An ex-smoker might be around someone smoking and have a nicotine reaction. All of a sudden, they have the urge to smoke a cigarette.[12]

Ready to Quit

Deciding to quit is an important first step. Choosing when is next. Counselors suggest circling a day on the calendar within thirty days.[13] It could be a birthday or anniversary, or another day with special meaning. That gives a person enough time to come up with a plan, but not so much time that he or she weakens and changes his or her mind.

Some people quit cold turkey. They choose a day and stop smoking or using chew all at once. Or they may cut down for the one or two weeks leading up to that day. But willpower alone sometimes is not enough. Other people quit gradually by using Nicotine Replacement Therapy (NRT)—such as nicotine gum, patches, or lozenges. These give off doses of nicotine without the other harmful chemicals in tobacco. Nicotine nasal spray and nasal inhalators are two other NRT options.

Current NRT options are not yet FDA-approved for teens, as safe dosage levels have not been adequately tested. As more studies are conducted, that may change. For now, public health guidelines recommend that healthcare providers counsel adolescents to stop smoking and to supplement with NRT if necessary.[14] Quit programs such as Not On Tobacco focus on changing behavior without the use of medication. Some in the medical community have recommended using NRT only in carefully selected cases, in combination with a stop-smoking program and under a doctor's supervision.[15]

All of the NRTs are supposed to help a person quit by gradually reducing the dose of nicotine.[16] The nicotine inhalator is shaped like a cigarette with a filter tip. Sucking on the mouthpiece releases nicotine vapor into a person's mouth and throat. It is to help people who want to quit but miss the hand-to-mouth action of smoking.

The nicotine patch provides a steady dose of nicotine, but may not help with strong cravings. It is useful for people who were heavy smokers and prefer the convenience of once-a-day application. The patch is also more discreet.

Quitting smokeless tobacco is a lot like quitting smoking. Both involve dealing with triggers and cravings. But former chew and snuff users tend to have a stronger craving for oral substitutes—like gum or hard candy.[17] For them, nicotine gum and lozenges may be more helpful.

People trying to quit have also tried hypnosis, acupuncture, and other chemical-free methods. Hypnosis works to free the mind's dependence on smoking as a habit. Acupuncture involves needles being inserted into pressure points to

98% OF GUYS WHO USE **CHEWING** TOBACCO SAY THEIR **MALE** FRIENDS DON'T MIND AT ALL*

*oddly, there are no figures for how their girlfriends feel about it.

CDC
CENTERS FOR DISEASE CONTROL AND PREVENTION

This antismoking ad from the Centers for Disease Control and Prevention shows that chewing tobacco is not a wise choice to make.

reduce cravings. No matter how someone tries to quit, experts agree that it may take repeated attempts to succeed.

Smart Choices

An easier alternative to quitting would be not to smoke or use chew in the first place. For some, that may be easier said than done. It is not always easy to resist pressure from friends. Some kids are simply curious to try something new and think that doing something forbidden will make them seem more mature. For many, the dizziness or nausea they feel the first time is enough to make it their last.

Those who think about trying again should speak to teens who have tried quitting. They typically wish that they had never started smoking. In fact, try asking a few of them how they would resist starting if they had it to do over again. Asking older peers who have never smoked how they turned down cigarettes could also be useful. They may have realistic suggestions.

It is important to recognize the impact of advertising. That is the reason many people start smoking: because an advertisement—or actor in a movie—made smoking look glamorous and attractive. Maybe the smoker in the ad or movie looks more confident than you feel or seems to be attracting more friends. In the words of the director of the World Health Organization, "The tobacco epidemic is a communicated disease. It is communicated through advertising, through the example of smokers and through

Teens do not need to use tobacco products to be popular.

the smoke to which nonsmokers—especially children—are exposed."[18]

Everyone has a choice in how they respond to advertising. They can be fooled by it or learn to see through it. The next time you see a tobacco ad, notice your emotional reaction to it. Think about what the company is trying to sell. Compare that fantasy with the reality of scientific research and health statistics. When it comes to tobacco advertising, some kids have actively worked to change where and how it is done.[19] For example, they have written to newspaper and magazine editors to voice their concerns, and persuaded stores to remove tobacco ads. Getting involved has not only empowered the teens, it also has helped to educate others.

Making smart choices now leads to a healthy life overall. If staying slim seems to be the appeal of smoking, choose a sport and learn about healthier eating. The time spent on smoking or chewing tobacco could be better used to improve a jump shot or running endurance. A beautiful body is a healthy and strong one. At the same time, improving diet and physical condition-ing relieves the stress that leads some to pick up a cigarette. In fact, despite short-term relief, tobacco actually increases long-term stress.[20]

If team sports are not appealing, take up something that can be done individually—skateboarding, jogging, or swimming, for example. In the off-season, try a different activity that has always seemed interesting. How about taking a drawing or painting class, singing lessons, or learning to play guitar or piano?

Do you have personal reasons for not using tobacco? Maybe it led to a relative's serious illness or death. Maybe you do not like the smell of smoke. Whatever the reasons, write them down and review them. The list may trigger more reasons. It also may reinforce your resolve to turn down a cigarette or chewing tobacco. Remember, most people choose not to smoke or use chew.

If a parent, brother, or sister smokes, make it a mission to learn all you can about the dangers—to them and to you, a passive smoker. Sharing the facts and statistics with current smokers in the family may encourage them to quit. Another smart choice.

GLOSSARY

acetylcholine—A neurotransmitter that regulates breathing, learning, memory, and movement.

addiction—A condition which compels someone to keep doing something, such as taking drugs or gambling, in a way that disrupts their life. With drug addiction, chemical changes develop in the brain.

adrenaline—Hormone secreted by the adrenal glands, which are just above each kidney, that increases blood pressure, heart rate, and respiration.

biopsy—A sample of body tissue taken to test for cancer and other diseases.

CAT scan—A form of X-ray. CAT stands for computerized axial tomography.

chronic bronchitis—A disease in which airways in the lungs change shape and size, and mucus glands enlarge to cause coughing and excess sputum.

cilia—Tiny hairlike structures that move mucus out of the lungs.

decapitation—Cutting off the head.

GLOSSARY

dopamine—A neurotransmitter that affects movement, emotions, motivation, and feelings of pleasure.

embalm—To preserve a body for funeral and burial.

emphysema—Incurable lung disease in which very small airways and air sacs are damaged. It makes breathing painful and difficult.

enzyme—Proteins that help chemical reactions happen more quickly. Without enzymes, our bodies would stop functioning.

esophagus—Tube connecting the mouth to the stomach.

larynx—Voice box.

lymph node—Fleshy pea-sized glands found in groups throughout the body. They are linked by special lymph channels that drain into the blood going to the right side of the heart.

neurotransmitter—Chemical messengers in brain.

nicotine—A chemical compound from the tobacco plant that is responsible for smoking's addictive effects. Toxic at high doses, it is used as medicine at lower doses.

NRT—Nicotine *replacement therapy*, which includes nicotine gum, patch, nasal spray, tablet, lozenge, and inhalator.

oral cavity—Region of the lip, tongue, mouth, and throat.

passive smoking—A nonsmoker's exposure to smoke (secondhand smoke) from a cigarette, cigar, or pipe.

secondhand smoke—Also called passive smoke and environmental smoke, it is a mixture of two types of smoke: Sidestream smoke comes from the cigar, cigarette, or pipe; and mainstream smoke is what the smoker exhales.

withdrawal—Symptoms that occur after stopping or reducing use of an addictive drug.

CHAPTER NOTES

Chapter 1. The Landscape

1. Personal interview with Officer John Wheeler, April 11, 2005.
2. Ibid.
3. Ibid.
4. Ibid.
5. "Nicotine," n.d., <http://encyclopedia.laborlawtalk. com/Nicotine> (April 2, 2005).
6. L. D. Johnstone, P. M. O'Malley, et al., "Decline in Teen Smoking Appears to be Nearing its End," *University of Michigan News and Information Services*, December 19, 2005, <http://www. monitoringthefuture.org> (February 9, 2006).
7. "Toxic Chemicals in Tobacco Products," n.d., <http://www.cdc.gov/tobacco/research_data/ product/objective21-20.htm> (February 17, 2006).
8. "Secondhand Smoke: Protect Yourself from the Dangers," n.d., <http://www.mayoclinic.com/ secondhand-smoke.htm> (February 10, 2006).
9. Alan I. Leshner, "Parents: Nicotine Is A Real Threat To Your Kids," National Institute on Drug Abuse, n.d., <http://www.drugabuse.gov/Published_Articles/ Nicotinethreat.html> (April 7, 2005).
10. "Child and Teen Tobacco Use," January 7, 2005, <http://www.cancer.org/docroot/PED/content/ PED_10_2X_Child_and_Teen_Tobacco_Use.asp? sitearea=PED> (March 3, 2005).
11. "Bidis and Kreteks," November 2005, <http:// www.cdc.gov/tobacco/factsheets/bidisandkreteks. htm> (December 14, 2005).

12. Ibid.
13. Ibid.
14. WHO Study Group on Tobacco Product Regulation (TobReg), *Waterpipe Tobacco Smoking: Health Effects, Research Needs and Recommended Actions by Regulators* (Geneva, Switzerland: World Health Organization, 2005), pp. 1–11.
15. "Where Do Kids Get Cigarettes?" November 26, 2004, <http://www.cancer.org/docroot/NWS/content/NWS_2_1X_Where_Do_Kids_Get_Cigarettes.asp> (March 17, 2005).
16. "UCSD Study Shows Number of Teens Who Start Smoking Each Day in U.S.," September 29, 1999, <http://www.ucsdnews.ucsd.edu/newsrel/health/addolsmoke.htm> (February 17, 2006).
17. T. Gansler, "Early Lifestyle Choices and Cancer," 2005, <http://www.cancer.org/docroot/PED/content/PED_11_1_Early_Lifestyle_Choices_and_Cancer.asp> (March 3, 2005).
18. "Teens and Smoking: What Parents Can Do," n.d., <http://www.mayoclinic.com/teen-smoking.htm> (February 9, 2006).
19. "Quitting Smokeless Tobacco," January 28, 2005, <http://www.cancer.org/docroot/PED/content/PED_10_13X_Quitting_Smokeless_Tobacco.asp.> (April 3, 2005).
20. "Cancer Facts," National Cancer Institute, May 30, 2003, <http://cis.nci.nih.gov/fact/10_15.htm> (March 3, 2005).
21. "Spit Tobacco: A Guide for Quitting," October 2004, <http://www.nidcr.nih.gov/HealthInformation/

OralHealthInformationIndex/SpitTobacco/Quitting Guide/> (April 12, 2005).

22. Ibid.

23. "Types of Smokeless (Spit) Tobacco," n.d., <http://www.intheknowzone.com/tobacco/spit_tobacco.htm> (February 23, 2005).

24. "Smokeless Tobacco: Especially for Kids" n.d., <http://www.dccps.nci.nih.gov/tcrb/less_kids.html> (February 17, 2006).

25. "Cigarette Smoking," January 6, 2005, <http://www.cancer.org/docroot/ped/content/ped_10_2x_cigarette_smoking.asp> (March 17, 2005).

26. "NIDA InfoFacts: Cigarettes and Other Nicotine Products," National Institute on Drug Abuse, March 2005, <http://www.drugabuse.gov/infofacts/tobacco.html> (April 7, 2005).

27. "Cigarette Smoking," January 6, 2005.

28. "WHO Framework Convention on Tobacco Control: Facts and Figures about Tobacco," February 6–17, 2006, <http://www.who.int/tobacco/fctc/cop/en/index.html> (February 9, 2006).

Chapter 2. Nicotine's Journey

1. Rochelle Schwartz-Bloom and Gayle Gross de Núñez, "The Dope on Nicotine," October 2001, <http://www.pbs.org/wgbh/nova/cigarette/nicotine.html > (April 9, 2005).

2. Ibid.

3. "Smokeless Tobacco," 2005, <http://www.cancer.org/docroot/PED/content/PED_10_2X_

Smokeless_Tobacco_and_Cancer.asp?sitearea=
PED> (March 3, 2005).

4. "Nicotine," National Institute on Drug Abuse, n.d.,
<http://teens.drugabuse.gov/facts/facts_
nicotine2.asp> (April 7, 2005).

5. Ibid.

6. Ibid.

7. Rochelle Schwartz-Bloom and Gayle Gross de
Núñez, "The Dope on Nicotine."

8. "Smokeless Tobacco," 2005.

9. Ibid.

10. "What is Nicotine?" n.d., <http://health.howstuff-
works.com/nicotine.htm> (February 17, 2005).

11. "Do You Know What You Are Smoking?" January
6, 2004, <http://www.hn.psu.edu/programs/
health/cig_chemicals.html> (April 11, 2005).

12. Ian Johnston, "Tobacco Companies 'Fooled'
Smokers," *The Scotsman*, February 8, 2006,
<http://news.scotsman.com/index.cfm?id=
197752006> (February 18, 2006).

13. "Cigarette Smoking," January 6, 2005, <http://
www.cancer.org/docroot/ped/content/ped_10_
2x_ cigarette_smoking.asp> (March 17, 2005).

14. Jessica Reaves, "An Important Ruling for Big
Tobacco," *Time*, March 21, 2000, <http://www.
time.com/time/nation/article/0,8599,41349,00.
html> (February 18, 2006).

15. "Cigarette Smoking," January 6, 2005.

16. "Smoking and the Environment," n.d.,
<http://www.smokefreeyouth.org/s04env.html>
(April 17, 2005).

17. Ibid.

18. Bridget M. Kuehn, "Link Between Smoking and Mental Illness May Lead to Treatments," *Journal of the American Medical Association*, vol. 295, no. 5, February 1, 2006, pp. 483–484.

19. Jeff Levine, "Study Concludes that Nicotine May Prevent Alzheimer's Disease," October 22, 1996, <http://www.cnn.com/health/9610/22/nfm/alzheimers/> (February 17, 2006).

Chapter 3. Nicotiana: One Plant's Story

1. Iain Gately, *Tobacco: The Story of How Tobacco Seduced the World* (New York: Grove Press, 2001), p. 3.

2. Gene Borio, "Tobacco Timeline," 2003, <http://www.tobacco.org/resources/history/Tobacco_History20-2.html> (February 17, 2005).

3. Ibid.

4. Ibid.

5. Gately, p. 118.

6. "Southern Tobacco In the Civil War," March 2002, <http://www.civilwarhome.com/tobacco.htm> (Apr 9, 2005).

7. Gately, p. 73.

8. Borio, "Tobacco Timeline," 2003.

9. Ibid.

10. Gately, p. 142.

11. Borio, "Tobacco Timeline," 2003.

12. "Southern Tobacco In the Civil War," March 2002.

13. Gately, p. 218.

14. Gordon L. Dillow, "Thank You For Not Smoking: The Hundred-Year War Against the Cigarette," *American Heritage Magazine*, vol. 32, February /March 1981, <http://www.americanheritage. com/articles/magazine/ah/1981/2/1981_2_94. shtml> (February 16, 2006).
15. Borio, "Tobacco Timeline," 2003.
16. Gately, p. 285.
17. Stanton Glantz, et al., *The Cigarette Papers* (Los Angeles: University of California Press, 1996), pp. 17, 39–40.
18. Ibid., p. 15.
19. Gately, p. 296.
20. "Warning Label," September 2005, <http:// www.cdc.gov/tobacco/sgr/sgr_2000/factsheets_ labels.htm> (February 16, 2006).
21. Gately, p. 310.
22. Borio, "Tobacco Timeline," 2003.
23. Report of the Surgeon General, *The Health Consequences of Smoking: Nicotine Addiction*, (U.S. Department of Health and Human Services: Washington, D.C., 1988), p. 9.
24. Glantz, et al., p. 1.
25. "Attorneys General Settlement Agreement," March 20, 1997, <http://stic.neu.edu/liggettsettle. htm> (February 17, 2006).
26. "Master Settlement Agreement Details," n.d., <http://www.streetheory.org/street/Content/ IssueArticlesFolder/IssueArticle.2003-01- 16.1605/issues_subportal> (April 11, 2005).
27. "State Tobacco Laws," December 27, 2004,

<http://www.cancer.org/docroot/PED/content/ PED_10_12_State_Legislated_Actions_on_Tobacco _Issues.asp?sitearea=PED> (April 7, 2005).

28. Borio, "Tobacco Timeline," 2003.

29. "Special Report: Justice Department Civil Lawsuit," March 8, 2005, <http://www. tobaccofreekids.org/reports/doj/> (April 8, 2005).

30. Christopher John Farley, "The Butt Stops Here," *Time*, April 18, 1994, <http://www.time.com/ time/archive/preview/0,10987,980572,00.html> (February 14, 2006).

31. "Chronology of Significant Developments Related to Smoking and Health," February 2006, <http://www.cdc.gov/tobacco/overview/chron96. htm> (February 17, 2006).

32. Ibid.

33. "Sports and Arts without Tobacco," n.d., <http://www.who.int/docstore/tobacco/ntday/ ntday96/pk96_5.htm> (February 17, 2006).

34. Borio, "Tobacco Timeline," 2003.

35. Ibid.

36. Poul Erik Petersen, "Tobacco and Oral Health: The Role of the World Health Organization," *Oral Health & Preventive Dentistry*, vol. 1, no. 4, Geneva, Switzerland, 2003, pp. 309–315.

37. "Tobacco Control Efforts Growing Worldwide as Countries Build on Momentum of Global Tobacco Convention," February 6, 2006, <http://www. who.int/mediacentre/news/releases/2006/pr07/ en/index.html> (February 9, 2006).

Chapter 4. Body of Evidence

1. Personal interview with Detective Sandra Oplinger, San Diego Police Department, March 23, 2005.
2. Ibid.
3. Personal interview with Dr. William Doyle, Brattleboro Memorial Hospital, April 25, 2005.
4. Ibid.
5. "Cancer-Lung Cancer Risk Factors," October 2005, <http://apps.nccd.cdc.gov> (February 15, 2006).
6. Personal interview with Dr. William Doyle, April 25, 2005.
7. John R. Polito, "Sean Marsee's Message," June 2000, <http://members.lycos.co.uk/zep_/whyquit/SeanMarsee.html?> (April 11, 2005).
8. Ibid.
9. Ibid.
10. Ibid.
11. Ibid.
12. "Smokeless Tobacco," November 2005, <http://www.cdc.gov/tobacco/factsheets/smokelesstobacco.htm> (February 15, 2006).
13. "Cigarette Smoking," January 6, 2005, <http://www.cancer.org/docroot/ped/content/ped_10_2x_cigarette_smoking.asp> (March 17, 2005).
14. Cynthia Kuhn, et al., *Buzzed: The Straight Facts About the Most Used and Abused Drugs From Alcohol to Ecstasy*, 2d ed. (New York: W.W. Norton & Co., 2003), p. 170.

15. Personal interview with Dr. William Doyle, April 25, 2005.

16. "Nicotine," National Institute on Drug Abuse, n.d. <http://teens.drugabuse.gov/facts/facts_nicotine1.asp> (April 7, 2005).

17. Ibid.

18. "Questions About Smoking, Tobacco, and Health," October 2004, <http://www.cancer.org/docroot/PED/content/PED_10_2x_Questions_About_Smoking_Tobacco_and_Health.asp?sitearea=PED> (April 3, 2005).

19. "Nicotine," National Institute on Drug Abuse.

20. "Smokeless Tobacco," 2005.

21. Kuhn, et al., p. 171.

22. "Peptic Ulcer," n.d., <http://www.mayoclinic.com/health/peptic-ulcer/ds00242/dsection=3> (February 17, 2006).

23. "Questions and Answers about Cigar Smoking and Cancer," n.d., <http://www.cancer.gov/cancertopics/factsheet/tobacco/cigars/> (February 15, 2006).

24. "Cigar Smoking," November 1, 2004, <http://www.cancer.org/docroot/PED/content/PED_10_2X_Cigar_Smoking.asp?sitearea=PED> (March 3, 2005).

25. Kuhn, et al., p. 173.

26. "Spit (Smokeless) Tobacco," 2005, <http://www.cancer.org/docroot/PED/content/PED_10_2X_Smokeless_Tobacco_and_Cancer.asp?sitearea=PED> (March 3, 2005).

27. "Types of Smokeless (Spit) Tobacco," n.d.

<http://www.intheknowzone.com/tobacco/spit_tobacco.htm> (February 23, 2005).

28. "Leukoplakia," November 2004, <http://www.mayoclinic.com/health/leukoplakia/> (February 10, 2006).

29. "Types of Smokeless (Spit) Tobacco."

30. "Smokeless Tobacco," 2005.

31. Ibid.

32. "Secondhand Smoke: Protect Yourself from the Dangers," n.d., <http://www.mayoclinic.com/health/secondhand-smoke/> (February 10, 2006).

33. Kuhn, et al., p. 171.

34. "Secondhand Smoke: Protect Yourself from the Dangers."

35. "Questions About Smoking, Tobacco, and Health," October 2004.

36. Elizabeth M. Whelan and Gilbert Ross, "The Growing Public Anxiety about Lung Cancer," April 8, 2005, <http://www.acsh.org/> (February 16, 2006).

37. "Secondhand Smoke," October 2004, <http://www.cancer.org/docroot/PED/content/PED_10_2X_Secondhand_Smoke-Clean_Indoor-air.asp?sitearea=PED> (March 3, 2005).

38. "Secondhand Smoke: Protect Yourself from the Dangers."

39. "Unbelievable But True Facts About ETS," Massachusetts Department of Public Health (ref: M. Males, JAMA, Jun 24, 1992, p. 3282), n.d. <http://www.getoutraged.com/> (April 7, 2005).

Chapter 5. The Anti-Social

1. Personal interview with Dr. Glenn Wagner, San Diego County Medical Examiner, April 21, 2005.
2. Ibid.
3. Personal interview with Officer John Wheeler, April 11, 2005.
4. Ibid.
5. Ibid.
6. Ibid.
7. "State Legislated Action on Tobacco Issues," February 2006, <http://slati.lungusa.org/statelegislateaction.asp> (February 15, 2006).
8. "Where Do Kids Get Cigarettes?" November 26, 2004, <http://www.cancer.org/docroot/NWS/content/NWS_2_1x_Where_Do_Kids_Get_Cigarettes.asp> (March 7, 2005).
9. Ibid.
10. Ibid.
11. Meg Gallogly, "The Path to Smoking Addiction Starts at Very Young Ages," January 10, 2005, <http://www.tobaccofreekids.org/research/factsheets/pdf/0127.pdf> (February 9, 2006).
12. L. D. Johnstone, P. M. O'Malley, et al., "Decline in Teen Smoking Appears to be Nearing its End," *University of Michigan News and Information Services*, December 19, 2005, <http://www.monitoringthefuture.org> (February 9, 2006).
13. "Secondhand Smoke: Cause for Concern," 2002, <http://www.tobaccofreeeu.org/secondhand_smoke/cause_for_concern.asp> (April 17, 2005).
14. Ibid.

15. Kimberly Yolton, et al., "Exposure to Environmental Tobacco Smoke and Cognitive Abilities among U.S. Children and Adolescents," *Environmental Health Perspectives*, vol. 113, no. 1, January 2005, pp. 98–103.
16. D. Turner-Baker and W. Hamilton, "Cigarette Advertising Expenditures Before and After Master Settlement Agreement: Preliminary Finding," Massachusetts Department of Public Health, 2000, <http://www.tobaccofreeu.org/facts_figures/index.asp> (April 17, 2005).
17. Charles King and Michael Siegel, "The Master Settlement Agreement with the Tobacco Industry and Cigarette Advertising in Magazines," *New England Journal of Medicine*, vol. 345, no. 7, August 16, 2001, pp. 504–511.
18. "Campaign Contributions By Tobacco Interests," January 2005, <http://tobaccofreeaction.net/contributions/> (April 9, 2005).

Chapter 6. Take Charge

1. Personal interview with Molly Gallegos and Carla Herried, April 28, 2005.
2. Ibid.
3. Ibid.
4. Ibid.
5. Ibid.
6. Ibid.
7. Ibid.
8. Ibid.
9. Ibid.

10. Ibid.

11. Personal interview with Steve Cordes, March 28, 2005.

12. Cynthia Kuhn, et al., *Buzzed: The Straight Facts About the Most Used and Abused Drugs From Alcohol to Ecstasy,* 2d ed. (New York: W.W. Norton & Co., 2003), p. 174.

13. "Quitting Spit (Smokeless) Tobacco," January 28, 2005. <http://www.cancer.org/docroot/PED/content/PED_10_13X_Quitting_Smokeless_Tobacco.asp.> (April 3, 2005).

14. Karen C. Johnson, et al., "Minors Able to Buy Nicotine Replacement Therapy Products," *Archives of Pediatrics & Adolescent Medicine*, vol. 158, March 2004, pp. 212–216.

15. William P. Adelman, "Nicotine Replacement Therapy for Teenagers," *Archives of Pediatrics and Adolescent Medicine*, vol. 158, March 2004, pp. 205–206.

16. "Quitting Smokeless Tobacco," January 28, 2005.

17. Ibid.

18. Gro Brundtland, "International Policy Conference on Children and Tobacco," World Health Organization, March 18, 1999, <http://www.who.int//director-general/speeches/1999/english/19990318_international_policy_conference.htm> (February 18, 2006).

19. Wendy S. Lesko, "Ask the Expert," January 2003, <http://www.streetheory.org> (February 17, 2006).

20. M. H. Milton, et al., *Youth Tobacco Cessation: A Guide for Making Informed Decisions,* (Atlanta: Centers for Disease Control and Prevention, 2004), p. 45.

FURTHER READING

Books

De Angelis, Gina. *Nicotine & Cigarettes.* Philadelphia, Penn.: Chelsea House Publishers, 2000.

Green, Carl. *Nicotine and Tobacco.* Berkeley Heights, N.J.: MyReportLinks.com Books, 2005.

Powell, Jillian. *Why Do People Smoke?* Austin, Tex.: Raintree Steck-Vaughn, 2001.

Silverstein, Alvin, Virginia Silverstein, and Laura Silverstein Nunn. *Smoking.* Franklin Watts, 2003.

Internet Addresses

Nicotine Addiction . . . and other dangers of tobacco use.
<http://smoking.drugabuse.gov>
Learn more about nicotine at this Web site from the National Institute on Drug Abuse.

You Can Quit Smoking Now!
<http://www.smokefree.gov/index.asp>
Get tips for quitting smoking at this Web site.

INDEX